The Amazing Journey of Lucky the Lobster Buoy

Karel Hayes

With love for my husband Brent,
whose passion for sailing brought us to
Penobscot Bay, where one summer I read
a small newspaper article about a lost
Maine lobster buoy found on a beach
in England.

Also this book is dedicated to the
memory of my parents, Sophia Murdza
Hayes and John Edward Hayes and all
our family's Down East summers.

ISBN (13-digit): 978-0-89272-791-9

Design by Lynda Chilton

Printed in China.

5 4 3 2 1

Down East
BOOKS·MAGAZINE·ONLINE
www.downeast.com

www.downeast.com
Distributed to the trade by National Book Network

Library of Congress Cataloging-in-Publication Date available on request

In a small boathouse at the edge of the Atlantic Ocean,
Tim, the son of a lobster fisherman, carved his first buoy
out of a block of wood.

He painted it red and green to match his father's buoys and added his phone number on the handle. Then he painted on the number 4. Four had always been his lucky number.

When his sister remarked that the rough surface of his buoy looked like a face, Tim added eyes and a mouth, and named the buoy Lucky.

Tim was very proud. He thought that a lobster buoy like no other had to be a lucky lobster buoy.

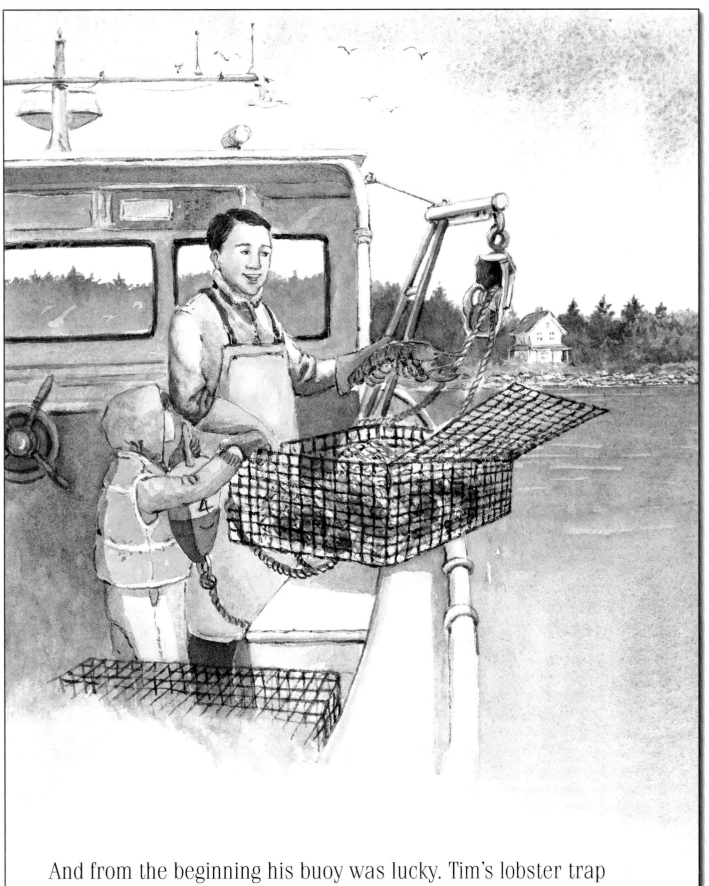

And from the beginning his buoy was lucky. Tim's lobster trap
was always full. His buoy was lucky all summer...

until one day at the end of August,

when Lucky's line was cut by a boat propeller.

Now Lucky was alone with the setting sun and the outgoing tide.

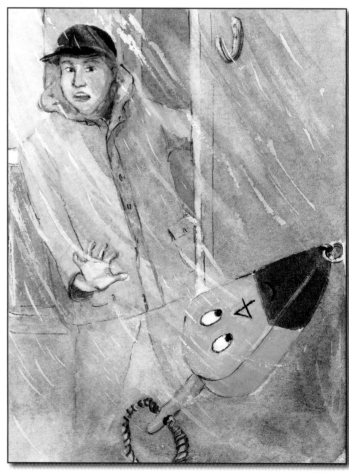

Lucky eventually made it back to Tim—
and retired from lobster fishing.

Tim often wondered about his buoy,

but he knew he would never
know all that happened to Lucky
on his amazing journey.

The End